Grynbad

AND THE SEVEN SOUPS

David Hailwood

Book 1 in the Grynbad Series

Biomekazoik Press

With thanks to Pete Lancaster for uttering the fateful words: "Did you know it's actually possible to run across the surface of custard..?"

Contents

An Unhealthy Appetite

There was only one thing in the entire world that I loved more than my Grandpa Grynbad, and that was his false teeth.

They were the biggest, widest, most magnificent set of gnashers ever to grace the grizzled lips of a senior citizen. Such was their size that his mouth was forced permanently open into the sort of wide, manic grin that would've made alligators dive for cover and hyenas stop laughing and go about their business.

And they gave him an appetite. Boy, what an appetite! Anything you could bite, gnaw, nibble or gnash fell beneath the might of those massive molars.

Every day at suppertime children came from all over the neighbourhood to press their noses against the window, and play their favourite game: 'Guess what Grandpa Grynbad's gonna gobble next?'

'Bet it's whalebone and woodchips,' yelled one.

'Nah. Wellies and ice cream!' suggested another.

'Hobnail boots with the feet still in.'

'Cement sandwiches,' cried a fourth. 'With extra gravelly gravy!'

My mother stormed to the window and scowled hard at their grubby faces. 'For your information, he's going to have a nice *soft* omelette.' She pulled the curtains shut.

'Pah!' spat Grandpa. 'Omelettes are for sissies! Give me something I can sink me teeth into.'

'Crocodile steak!' I cried, banging my knife and fork on the table.

'Ooh yeah, that's a good one,' said Grandpa, smacking his lips. 'Tough as shoe leather, and hard as nails.'

'Or bricks,' I suggested, gnashing my teeth. 'Nice crunchy bricks.'

'Now yer talkin' lad. Been years since I had a nice brick an' butter pudding.'

Mum waggled a stern finger under Grandpa's nose. 'You're a bad influence on the boy. Tell him, Harold.'

Dad looked briefly up from his newspaper. 'Oh, he's all right really,' he said. 'Let him have his fun.'

'He should be in a home!'

'He is in a home,' said Dad.

'A different home. One where we're not.'

Dad massaged his forehead with the tips of his fingers. 'Not this again, Helen…'

'*Show us yer teeth! Show us yer teeth! Show us yer teeth!*' chanted the kids from outside.

'Hark! What's this? A curtain call?' said Grandpa, feigning surprise. 'Will you excuse me a moment, Timothy? My audience awaits.' Grandpa left the table and brushed haughtily past mother, hobbling towards the curtain.

'Don't even think about it, you crusty old—'

In one swift motion he pulled back the curtain and thrust his glistening chops against the window. 'Mmm! Bite-sized boys and gristly girls!' he yelled, chomping and gnashing his teeth like a blood-crazed badger. 'My favourite!'

The children scattered, shrieking and whooping and laughing with glee.

Grandpa turned to me and gave a cheery wink. 'That showed them, eh Timothy?'

'It certainly did, Grandpa.' I gave him my toothiest, yellowest, gappiest grin.

Mum stared at it in horror, and said those words that every child dreads. 'It's the dentists for you in the morning, my boy.'

Grandpa Grynbad Meets His Match

The crumbling archway of King Clancy's Home For Wayward Old Rascals loomed over us out of the undergrowth like a giant brick beast.

Our trip to the dentists had not gone well.

'He's rattling again,' said Mum as her car thundered past it, and continued up the long, winding driveway.

'Oh, that's probably just the carburetor or something,' said Dad, feigning knowledge in an area that he had none.

'It's him.' Mum scowled hard at the crusty old man reflected in her rear-view mirror. 'He's rattling.'

'It's just me teeth,' said Grandpa Grynbad. 'They always rattle when I'm on edge.'

'And whose fault is that?' Mum scolded. 'We warned you this would happen. You're a bad influence on young Timothy.'

I attempted to give Grandpa a brave smile, but my face was so numb from the dentist's injection that I looked like a hunchback posing for a passport photo.

'I don't see what all the fuss is about,' said Grandpa sulkily. 'It was only ten fillings. I had twice that when I was Timmy's age, and it didn't do me no harm.'

'No harm?' Mum glared at Grandpa in the rear-view mirror. 'You don't have any teeth!'

'Oh yeah?' said Grandpa, whipping out his chompers and waving them around. 'Waddaya call theesh?'

After a bit of swerving, and a lot of crashing, we left the car parked in a hedge, and continued the journey on foot.

'You'll like it here,' said Dad, as we passed a well-stocked graveyard that sat opposite the old people's home. 'It's got a view.'

At that moment, a band of gap-toothed urchins leapt out from behind the gravestones and began to chant: *'Show us yer teeth! Show us yer teeth! Show us yer teeth!'*

'Ooh, must be suppertime already,' said Grandpa, grinding his teeth at his eager young audience. 'No wonder me gobblers are gaspin'.'

Their playful laughter turned to shrieks as something tall, dark and sinister stalked towards them from the door to the old people's home. 'Begone, younglings!' the terrifying apparition screeched. 'It is not your time. Return to me when you are old, withered and unloved. Then we will have much to discuss.'

As they fled, the figure turned its baleful red eyes upon us.

I hid behind Dad, who hid behind Mum, who gave him a clout round the ear.

'I am Miss Skillet,' the perilously thin figure announced, her long, sinuous shadow cleaving a gap between us and Grandpa. 'Custodian of the old and unruly.' She patted her jet-black hair bun, which had been tied back so tightly that it took much of her forehead with it. 'Let it be known that I run a tight ship.'

'Ghost ship crewed by the damned, more like,' mumbled Grandpa, giving her one of his looks.

'Is this the one?' she asked, squinting down her glasses at Grandpa.

'Oh, he's a one alright,' said Mum. 'Good luck with him.'

'Mr Grynbad.' Miss Skillet's pale, thin lips curled upwards into a sneer. 'You are most fortunate to come my way at your time of life. Most fortunate indeed.'

'Eh?' said Dad, who hadn't been paying attention.

'I was addressing Mr Grynbad senior,' clarified Miss Skillet. 'The elderly are well looked after here. Never again will you need to lift a finger, for within these fair walls a life of luxury awaits.' She wrapped a bony arm around Grandpa's shoulder, dug in her nails and swept him inside.

''Ere, what time's supper?' asked Grandpa as he hobbled down a dark, drab corridor that looked and smelt like a sickly cat's litter tray.

Miss Skillet led us towards a cavernous dining area, where the air was thick with the wet, sloppy sound of several dozen pensioners slurping in unison. Had a thousand burly farmers filled their wellies with porridge and vigorously stomped up and down in quicksand, the noise they created would've been nothing compared to this.

The sight was worse. Soup dribbled down chins, and gathered in beards, only to be strained out and shovelled back into that vast glistening empire of gummy mouths. At their sides, each pensioner had a glass of water in which false teeth bobbed uselessly up and down like starving piranhas.

'You're in luck,' said Miss Skillet, giving Grandpa a ghoulish grin. 'It's steak night. Won't that be a treat?'

Grandpa peered into the dark gloomy depths of one of those frightful dishes. 'Looks more like soup to me.'

'Yes,' Miss Skillet beamed, 'steak soup. A popular choice.'

'Don't like soup,' sniffed Grandpa. 'It turns me innards runny. Give me somethin' I can sink me teeth into.'

'Oh heavens, no,' Miss Skillet chuckled. 'You won't be needing those unsightly objects here. All the chewing's done for you. For, you see, we have a machine!'

We followed her long striding legs into a dank, oily room full of clanking pistons and whirring gears.

'Behold!' cried Miss Skillet, throwing her arms out wide. 'The Gnashomatic 4500!'

Before us, an assortment of hardy food produce such as Scottish spuds, ostrich eggs, tortoise toes and walruses' kneecaps, rumbled along a conveyor belt towards a massive set of towering metal munchers that put Grandpa's teeth to shame. Everything they encountered was gnashed, mashed, gobbled up and spat out into barrels labelled 'Breakfast', 'Lunch' and 'Supper'.

In her excitement, Miss Skillet began to prance up and down, singing a little song.

'No more miserable munching for you!

Never again will you need to chew!

It's what the Gnashomatic was born to do!

It's an eldster's greatest dream come true!'

'Nightmare, more like,' grumbled Grandpa. 'What's the point of having the world's greatest gobblers if there's nothing for me to sink them into?'

'Second greatest, I think you'll find,' corrected Miss Skillet, staring fondly at her precious machine.

'Stone the crows!' exclaimed Dad suddenly. 'There's a bloke over there floating around in custard!'

'Oh that's probably just the Major, back from one of his little expeditions,' said Miss Skillet. 'Out you get now Major. We have visitors.'

A short, dumpy man with a massive bristling moustache squelched out of a barrel, slopped onto the floor and squidged off a salute. 'Hunting Gribble Grobbles, dontcherknow?'

'What's a Gribble Grobble?' I asked.

'Dastardly yellow beasts. Cowards to a man! And where do you find cowards, lad? Custard!' The Major scraped a few congealing lumps off his safari outfit, and squished them in his fists. 'But never fear, I'll flush the blighters out, just you wait and see.'

'Well, good luck with that,' said Mum, making for the door. 'Time we were heading off.'

'You can't leave me here with these nutters,' Grandpa hollered, as I was whisked from the building and off towards the car. 'I'll go all peculiar.'

'No you won't,' said Dad.

'Yes I will!' insisted Grandpa fiercely. 'You just try and stop me!'

3

Grabbed By The Gribble Grobbles

The phone rang early the next morning, disturbing me from a rather unpleasant dream I'd been having about a tooth fairy armed with a chainsaw.

'Uh-huh? Yes? I see,' said Dad's voice from downstairs. 'A Gribble Grobble, you say? Well, thanks for letting us know. We'll be over as soon as we can.'

'What's wrong?' I asked, leaping down the stairs three at a time.

'Bad news, I'm afraid,' said Dad, putting the phone back on the hook. 'Your Grandpa's gnashers have been grabbed by a great green Gribble Grobble.'

I stared at him in amazement, unable to blink or breathe. Could Grandpa really have been so careless as to let his most prized possession be snatched from his jaws by a custard dwelling menace?

'I always thought Gribble Grobbles were yellow,' said Mum, as she emerged from the kitchen with a well-stacked tray of toasted tea-cakes.

'Yes, they're a crafty breed all right.' Dad settled down on the sofa, and reached for something to munch on. 'Any chance of a cuppa to go with this, my passion?'

After I'd dressed and my parents had finished breakfast, elevenses, and brunch, we headed to the old people's home where we found Grandpa still sat at the dining table, gloomily staring at an upturned bowl of custard. Without those glorious great dentures to prop his mouth wide open he was a sorry sight. His face looked like a punctured prune, and the rest of his body had wilted around it.

'What on earth were you doing trying to eat custard, Grandpa?' I scolded.

He turned his tortured eyes upon me, and sobbed: 'It wash the only food I could find with lumpsh in. Turnsh out, one of them lumpsh wash a Gribble Grobble in dishguishe.'

'I warned you!' cried the Major, hopping up and down on the table. 'Oh, how I warned you!'

'Get down from there, you old rascal.' Miss Skillet clapped her hands at the back of the Major's heels, and then turned her attention to Grandpa. 'Of course, none of this would have happened if you'd removed the offending article before tucking into your meal, as is strictly stated in—'

'Oh, tell her to get losht,' said Grandpa.

'Sorry? Afraid I didn't quite catch that,' said Miss Skillet, smiling sweetly.

'You shee?' cried Grandpa. 'I'm nothing without me teesh.'

'Well then, there's only one thing for it,' declared the Major. 'We must get after them at once.'

He dashed from the room, and returned moments later wheeling a large barrel of custard.

'Well?' he said, giving me an expectant look. 'In you get then.'

'*Me?*' I cried, shrinking away from the murky yellow muck. 'Why me? *You're* the expert.'

'He's your Grandpa,' said the Major. 'I've only just met the man. Can't go round questing for teeth of people I've only just met. Wouldn't be proper!'

'Hurry, lad,' urged Grandpa. 'If I don't get shomething to bite shoon I'll shrivel away to dusht.'

That pleading look in Grandpa's eyes was all I needed to spur me onwards. I plunged headfirst into the barrel of custard, and sat there a moment, squelching around, feeling a little foolish.

'Now what?' I asked.

'Now we stir!' cried the Major, producing a large wooden spoon from behind his back. 'Stir with all our might.'

He thrust in the spoon and waggled it with vigour.

Dad grabbed hold of the end (always happy to help stir a good custard), and round and round and round it went.

They stirred harder and harder, and faster and faster, creating a vast sucking yellow whirlpool from which there was no escape.

As I was dragged under into its gloopy depths I heard my mother shout: 'Don't forget to brush your teeth!'

Then I was gone, swept away on fierce custard currents.

4

Pea Soup Pirates

When I resurfaced sometime later, there was custard in my ears, eyes, and a few other places I'd rather not mention.

Once the yellow haze had cleared from my vision, I glanced around at my surroundings and found myself in a strange land of liquid. Vast rolling waves of custard stretched out in all directions, and a sizzling red sun baked me from above.

As I bobbed up and down in the gloopy waters, watching yellow-speckled gulls scooping lumps from the custard, a rather troublesome thought occurred to me; I didn't actually know what a Gribble Grobble looked like, or where they lived, or how to swim in custard.

Then I began to sink, back down into that murky yellow mire. I thrashed and I kicked, but it was no use. Custard sucked at me like an old man's gums. First it took my shoes, and then it took my socks. I felt it tugging at my trousers, and decided that enough was enough!

If I couldn't swim in custard I'd just have to learn to walk on it.

I'd heard somewhere that if you got up enough speed you could run across its surface without falling in. Since I was currently drowning, I really had very little to lose. I clawed my way upwards onto a thin crusty layer of skin, and spread myself out, attempting to evenly distribute my weight. Slowly, carefully, I got to my knees…

And then to my feet…

Next, I took a cautious, wobbling step…

Then another…and another…

And then…

Then I was running! Running as fast as the custard would carry me.

Oh, how I skimmed across its surface, speeding along like some wild, crazed thing. Yellow slime dribbled down my cheeks and squished between my toes, but I did not care because I was young and free and running on custard!

My confidence grew; I tried a cartwheel, a handstand, a pirouette, a flip. I was the Custard King, bane of the Gribble Grobble. Nothing could stop me now, not even razor-sharp raisin rocks or killer custard crabs.

That is, of course, the problem with a really good custard; just as you're starting to enjoy it, it's over.

And over I certainly went, all right. Straight over the edge of a mighty Custard Falls, legs whirring uselessly away in the air, until—

SPLOSSSSH!

I plunged into the tepid soupy waters below.

I clung a moment to a giant pea, and contemplated my fate.

Was it possible, I wondered, to run across the surface of pea soup? Perhaps I didn't need to. Unlike custard, this soup was thin and runny. My legs were tired, but my arms still had strength.

So I swam onwards through the mist that coiled around me, wondering what horrors lay within.

I didn't have to wait long to find out.

A ship emerged, churning its way through the waters with thick soupspoon oars. A black skull and crossbones flag grinned at me from the mast.

Pea soup pirates!

Before I could turn tail and flee, I was hoisted from the waters and found myself star-ing up into a collection of unwashed, grizzled faces, one of which had the whitest, most perfect set of teeth ever to have adorned the mouth of a pirate.

'Arrrr!' said the white-toothed pirate Captain. 'Be you man or crouton?'

'I'm a boy, actually,' I admitted.

The pirates lowered their spoons, which they'd been waving in the air like cutlasses, and grumbled in disappointment.

'Then what in the name o' Neptune's knickers were ye doin' floatin' around in soup?' snapped the Captain.

I put my hands on my hips, and struck up a heroic pose. 'Hunting Gribble Grobbles, dontcherknow?'

'Yer way off course fer Gribble Grobbles,' said the Captain. 'They dwell within the deep, dark depths of minestrone – everyone knows that.'

'I always thought they lived in custard,' mumbled one pirate.

'No, custard's where they hunt,' replied another. 'Minestrone's where they make their lair.'

The Captain leant forward and fixed me with his one good eye. 'What business have you with those accursed soup devils?'

'They stole the false teeth of someone very dear to me.'

'And now yer thirsty fer vengeance, eh? Well, it looks like you have a long and perilous journey ahead,' said the Captain. 'For you must cross the Seven Soups, brave the foul reekin' depths of minestrone, slay the beast, claim yer prize an' win back the heart of yer fair toothless maiden.'

'Um, they're my Grandpa's teeth, actually.'

The boisterous cries of the crew faded in an instant.

The pirate Captain stared at me as he attempted to digest this new nugget of information. 'In that case, I shouldn't bother,' he said with a shrug. 'Go home and play on your Nintendo.'

'But my Grandpa needs to eat.'

'He can always get more teeth.'

'Not like these,' I said, misty-eyed from the memory. 'They're absolute whoppers.'

'That may be so lad, but I'll bet they're no substitute for the real McCoy!' The Captain opened his mouth wide, and gave me a toothy grin.

I had to admit, they were the shiniest, whitest, most dazzling set of teeth I'd ever had the privilege to encounter. I began to wonder what his secret was.

'Mulch maggots!' said the Captain suddenly.

'I beg your pardon?'

'I've seen that look in yer eyes before,' grinned the Captain. 'You were wondering how I got such perfect white teeth.'

'Mulch maggots?'

'Arrr! Mulch maggots.' The Captain rummaged around in his beard, and pulled out a handful of wriggling little beasts. 'Apply liberally to yer chompers at night, and when you wake in the morning they'll have picked 'em clean.' That ghastly maggoty hand was thrust keenly in my direction. 'Go on, give 'em a try – they're minty fresh.'

'No fear!' I wrinkled my nose in disgust.

With an understanding nod, the Captain returned the maggots to the safety of his beard. 'Don't like the taste of mint, eh? Well, if yer won't take my maggots, at least take my advice. If you're to stand any chance of survivin' the perils that await ye, any chance at all, you're gonna need...a boot.'

'A boat?' My heart leapt. I couldn't believe my luck. Was this kindly old Captain truly going to lend me a boat?

'No, lad,' said the Captain. 'A *boot!*' And with that, he planted his foot firmly against my rump and kicked me back into the ocean.

'Don't forget to tell all yer friends Captain Crabcakes is a right old stinker!' cackled the dastardly pirate, as he sailed away into the mist.

5

Fishy Footwear

Down I sank through the soup's gloomy depths, until I came to a rest at the bottom, knee-deep in mushy peas. Strange creatures squelched at me from within, watching with curious eyes.

Some of their eyes were a little too curious for my liking, and their mouths a little too ravenous.

Time, I thought, to return to the surface.

Suddenly I caught sight of something that almost took my breath away; a brown leathery shoal of boots were marching across the bed of peas, their laces trailing majestically out behind them.

To think, it had never occurred to me that the reason people find so many boots in canals is simply because that's where they come from; it's their natural habitat. The answer was so obvious that I must confess I felt a little foolish for not realising so before.

Something else that suddenly occurred to me was that Captain Crabcakes might have been telling the truth. What I needed was a boot! Two boots, in fact. With a pair of seafaring soup boots on my feet I could stride gracefully across the waves and reach my destination in no time.

I stayed motionless so as not to alarm them, and singled out a weedy-looking pair that were straggling at the back.

In one swift movement I snatched the boots as they passed, forced them onto my feet, and tied the laces before they could wriggle free.

Once they'd stopped thrashing around and resigned themselves to their fate as footwear, I lifted a foot and inspected my prize. It was the ugliest boot I'd ever worn, full of barnacles and itchy patches of moss.

Still, they were all I had, so I'd just have to make do. 'Up, up and away!' I cried, my voice bubbling away in the soup.

The boots just stood there, shuffling nervously.

'Up!' I commanded once more. 'That way! Go!'

After rocking me back and forth on their heels for a moment, the boots finally reached a decision, and lurched off across the mushy green seabed.

This was no good at all. I had hoped to stride boldly across the waves, not squelch along below them.

'Up,' I cried. 'Up! Up!'

But it was useless; the boots had a new owner to break in, and they were going to try him out until they were satisfied.

After much stomping and squelching, the waters changed from dull green to a dazzling silver-grey.

I'd left the murky depths of pea soup behind and entered the colourful and vibrant realm of fish soup.

All around me exotic creatures darted and swirled, shimmering and glistening.

Red-nosed clownfish honked out a greeting as they unicycled past, juggling sea anemones; soft-bellied soup squids squirted elegantly through the waters, giving the soup its creamy flavour, and self-important celebrity starfish swaggered along, followed by a grovelling entourage of clapping clams.

Such beauty! Such majesty! Such —

STOMP! SMASH! CRUNCH! CRASH!

My ugly great pea soup clodhoppers ploughed right through the middle of them, smashing down seahorses' stables and kicking their way through king crabs' kingdoms.

'Sorry! My fault!' I cried. 'New shoes. Just trying them for size.'

A king crab's mandibles clacked angrily away beneath his golden crown, and within moments my feet were set upon by hordes of angry snapping pincers.

It seemed I was fast becoming a bigger menace than Gribble Grobbles.

'Up!' I commanded, with even greater urgency. 'Up! Up!'

The boots, who were perhaps tired of being poked and prodded by enraged crustaceans, finally saw reason. Up they soared through the bubbling waters, dragging me along helplessly behind them – feet first, and upside down.

I shot to the surface like a rocket, and landed in a crumpled heap on a large bread crust island.

Three mermaids lay upon it, basking in the sun.

They weren't as beautiful as those I'd read about in stories. Lank green strands of seaweed dangled from their scalps, huge fish-lips protruded from their faces, and a strange smell like rancid tuna hung in the air.

They stared at me a moment, and then slowly transferred their gaze to my boots.

'New shoes! New shoes!' they squealed.

Before I could react, the mermaids pounced on me and wrestled the boots from my feet.

'This one's mine!' cried the fattest of the trio.

'This one's mine!' cried the ugliest.

'Hey!' cried the eldest, frantically scrabbling at my bare feet. 'Where's *my* shoe?'

I pushed her off and brushed myself down. 'I only have two, and they're both mine. That's why I was wearing them.'

'Too late!' cackled the fattest mermaid, as she attempted to force her oversized tail into the trembling boot. 'We're wearing them now.'

'You'll never fit in there, sister,' scorned the eldest mermaid. 'Give it to me. Let me try.'

'I'll…fit…' grunted the fat mermaid. 'I'm a…size…zero!'

With a sickening *'Shhhlocck!'* she scrunched her bloated tail into the boot.

'Aha! See? Told you!' She hopped awkwardly towards me, wincing with every step. 'Tell me truthfully now,' she said, batting her watery eyelids. 'How do I look?'

'Like a big fat fish stuck in a shoe,' I said.

The mermaid's eyes blazed with fury. *'Whattt?'* she screeched.

'I said you look delightful,' I hastily amended.

'He was right the first time,' sniggered the eldest mermaid. 'You both look ridiculous.'

The ugliest mermaid, who'd also managed to squeeze herself into one of the boots, wobbled from side to side, like a big fishy Weebil. 'How do you people move in these things?'

'We use our feet,' I said, wiggling my bare toes.

'Aha! So that's your little secret is it?' cried the eldest mermaid triumphantly.

'The secret of the shoes! The secret of the shoes!' chanted her two sisters.

'Come now, sisters,' commanded the eldest, 'let us grow feet.'

They lay on their backs like beached whales, gasping, groaning and straining away.

'Hnnngggggggh! *Hnnnnnnnnggggghhhhhh!*'

'What are you doing?' I asked after a while.

'Attempting…to evolve…feet,' scowled the eldest mermaid. 'It's…happened before, it can…happen…again.'

'Won't that take rather a long time?' I observed.

The straining stopped. The mermaids exchanged glances.

'He's right, you know,' grumbled the eldest. 'By the time we've evolved feet, those shoes will be well out of fashion. We need feet, and we need them now.'

'Hang on a moment,' said the ugliest mermaid thoughtfully. '*He's* got feet.'

'Yes! Yes!' cried the fattest mermaid, rubbing her hands craftily together. 'And we already know the shoes are a perfect fit.'

Again I was leapt upon, and the mermaids' scaly fingers yanked violently at my feet, twisting and turning.

'Give them to us,' they pleaded. 'Give us your feet!'

'Stop tugging. Please! They're not meant to come off.'

'We'll soon see about that,' cried the fattest, pinning me down with her blubbery body. 'Sisters, fetch me the swordfish!'

As two of the mermaids flopped off down the crusty beach, I seized my moment and lashed out with all my strength.

'Argh!' cried the fattest mermaid, stumbling backwards. 'Kicked in the face by my own impending feet. Cruel fate, cruel fate.'

Free from her grasp, I dashed frantically towards the crust's edge.

'Stop running,' the mermaids called after me. 'Those are *our* feet you're using. We forbid it!'

Ignoring their despairing cries I plunged into the soup, and swam as fast as I could, shoeless, but thankful to still have feet.

'Ooh look at them go,' said the fattest mermaid wistfully. 'I bet I'd have looked great in those...'

6

Tomato Soup Troll Booth

The waters changed once more, from silvery-grey to a thick blood-red.

What foul, bloodthirsty creatures lurked in such depths, I wondered?

Wait! What was that? Had something brushed against my foot?

I thrashed around in panic, splashing soup into my mouth. I was surprised to discover it was warm, creamy and pleasant to the taste. Relief washed over me. I was on safe, familiar ground.

Surely nothing bad could possibly happen to me in good, honest tomato soup?

As I swam on, sweat formed on my brow. Further still, and steam began to rise from my skin. Boy, this tomato soup sure was hot.

A little *too* hot…

I was being boiled alive!

There was nothing else for it – I'd have to turn back, stick to the edge, and avoid the middle (which, as everyone knows, is the hottest part).

But which way did the edge lie?

I scanned the horizon, and saw nothing but thick red soup in all directions.

Then something caught my eye; a long line of massive slab-like croutons, delicately arranged like stepping-stones. Scale one of those, and I could hop from crouton to crouton, avoiding the blistering heat of the soup.

I scrambled up the jagged side of the crouton closest to me, and slowly began to work my way across the line.

The croutons were as sharp as blades beneath my bare feet. To make matters worse, some of them crumbled at the edge as I approached. One crouton disintegrated the moment I set foot on it, and I was forced to hurriedly fling myself towards the next.

Tomato soup hissed and spat at me from the waters below. If I fell in now, I'd melt away to nothing in an instant.

Slowly I continued onwards, until I could go no further. My path ahead was blocked by a barrier connected to a tollbooth, which hung precariously out over the crouton's side, supported by breadstick scaffolding. A fat blue sea troll was sat inside the booth, flicking boogers at a dartboard.

'Three clams, mate,' he said, as I approached.

'I'm sorry?'

The troll looked at me with bored eyes, and gnashed his yellow teeth. 'If you want to get past the barrier, it'll cost you three clams.'

'Why?'

'Maintenance costs. Croutons crumble, yer know? Takes a lot of clams to keep the crossing running.'

'Well you're not doing a very good job,' I grumbled. 'I almost fell in twice.'

'You're right, you're right, you're absolutely right,' said the troll. 'Five clams, please.'

'You said it was three a moment ago.'

'Like you said, gotta keep the crossing chugging along. Seven clams.'

'I don't have any clams.'

'Then you'll have to go back the way you came. Plenty of clams back in fish soup.'

I glanced back along the long, hazardous road of croutons. My feet were sore, my fingers blistered.

'I can't go back,' I said, shaking my head in defiance. 'One of the croutons crumbled behind me. I'd never make it across.'

'Which is why it's absolutely essential that you and other users contribute towards the maintenance costs,' the troll's monotonous voice droned. 'Twelve clams.'

'This is hopeless.'

'You could always take your chances in the waters below,' the troll suggested. 'Swimming costs nothing.'

I peered down at the soup, bubbling away below me like the mouth of a volcano. 'I'd be boiled alive!'

'I don't make the rules, mate,' said the troll, with a shrug. 'Now, are you sure you don't have any clams? Your pockets look nicely stuffed.'

'Yes,' I growled, 'stuffed full of custard!' I turned a pocket inside out, and thrust the gloopy yellow contents towards the troll. 'I came through a whole ocean of it, and a lot more besides just to —'

Suddenly, a hideous green tentacle lashed out from the custard, snatched the troll's teeth from out of his gaping mouth, and vanished back into the squelchy lining of my pocket.

We both stared at it, aghast.

All that time I'd spent searching for Gribble Grobbles, and there was one right there in my pocket, lying in wait. They certainly were a cunning breed, and no mistake!

''Ere,' said the troll, once he'd come to his senses, 'you did that on purposhe!'

'Don't worry, I'll get your teeth back for you, if you'll just let me past.'

Grumbling and moaning, the troll reluctantly raised the barrier. 'Go on then, find me my teesh. I need them to eat all the clamsh.'

I ducked under the barrier, and scowled back at the toothless troll. 'You *eat* the clams?'

''Coursh I do,' said the troll shamelessly. 'A trollsh belly takesh a lot of maintenansh too, you know. Now go on, get!'

7

Feeding Time In The Oxtail Swamp

I sat upon the final crouton on the crossing, dangling my legs over the heaving brown sludge below. What manner of soup was this, I wondered grimly?

It smelt worse than a mermaid's laundry basket, and vast clouds of bloated flies buzzed across its surface. All that kept me from turning back was the thought that if I made it safely across, I'd be more than half way towards my goal.

I took a deep breath, held my nose and prepared to take the plunge…

Suddenly, a feathery pair of hands reached up out of the soup. I watched in astonishment as a huge six-foot tall chicken clawed its way up the crouton and sat down beside me, soaked through and stinking.

'Trust me, mate,' said the chicken, as he turned his beak towards me, 'you do *not* want to go that way.'

I noticed a zipper running down the chicken's back, and realised he was merely a man in a chicken outfit. Well, it would take more than the words of a man dressed as poultry to stop me in my quest. 'I'm afraid I have no choice,' I replied.

The chicken man enveloped me with a tatty wing, and drew me in close. 'You see that?' he hissed, motioning to the murky brown waters. 'That's oxtail soup, lad. And you know what that means, don't you?'

I shook my head.

'Manotaurs!'

'Minotaurs?'

'No – Manotaurs! Much more fearsome. They've got the body of a cow, the legs of a cow, the tail of a cow, and the head...' he paused a moment as if trying to remember, and then continued: '...of a cow.'

'So, a cow then?' I said.

'Aye, but a big one though,' said the chicken man gruffly. 'She'd swallow you in a heartbeat.'

'I'll be sure to keep an eye out.' I scrambled down into the soup, and left the chicken man flapping around, clucking out his warnings from the crouton.

'Don't drink the soup, steer clear of mushrooms, and if you run into a Manotaur, tell her you're a chicken. It worked for me.'

His voice faded away into the gloom.

I waded onwards through the stagnant soup, flies biting every part of me that was exposed above the waters. The soup was shallower than I'd expected, and only came up to my armpits. This was very fortunate indeed, as the stench was enough to send my nostrils reeling. I kept my mouth tightly closed in a desperate attempt to avoid swallowing anything unpleasant.

Although the smell of the soup was bad, worse was yet to come.

It came in the form of a giant cowpat.

When I say giant, I mean **GIANT!** This monstrosity could've sunk a battleship.

Holding my breath, I carefully made my way past the unhygienic item, only to find myself confronted by another, and another. They were everywhere. Hundreds of steaming great cowpats, floating on top of the soup.

I bobbed and weaved through the waters, occasionally finding my path ahead blocked, forcing me to seek another way around (I could have tried ducking under the cowpats, but if I

resurfaced at the wrong moment the conse-
quences would've been disastrous).

Finally, I chanced upon their creator.

An obese, filth-encrusted cow lay wallowing
in the muck, folds of blubber rippling away like
great flabby waves.

'Ah,' said the Manotaur, turning its dour
yellow eyes upon me, 'you have made it
through my maze of cowpats. You must be very
stern of heart, and strong of stomach.'

'Id wad a doddle,' I said, holding my nose.
The creature reeked more than the foul offer-
ings it had left in its wake.

'Perhaps you'd care to rest a while, and
partake in a wholesome milky beverage?'
With considerable effort, the Manatour rolled
onto its back, and hefted its crusty udders at
me.

'I'b fide, thangs.'

'Well then, how about a milkshake?' The Manotaur thrashed, wobbled and gyrated her gigantic flabby body, sending a tsunami of soup crashing down over my head.

Once the waters had stopped swirling I resurfaced, coughing up oxtail and goodness knows what else.

'Refreshed?' asked the Manotaur.

I nodded frantically, not wishing to be hit by another wave of filth.

'Then let us get down to business. Before I grant you passage through my lair, you must pass a small series of simple tasks which I have named "Madam Daffodil's Three Thousand Five Hundred And Seventy Six Incredibly Complex Challenges!"'

'Do I have to?' I grumbled.

'I suppose not,' the Manotaur shrugged. 'Though it does mean you won't get a sticker.'

'I can live without a sticker.'

'Okay, if you're sure.' The Manotaur tucked a large napkin under one of her many folds of flab, and wallowed towards me, smacking her lips. 'Right, if you'd be so good as to make your own way down. I can't be bothered with all that energetic "chewing" business.' She opened her mouth wide and motioned with a hoof towards the vast gaping chasm that lay within.

'Why would I do that?' I asked, backing away.

'It's what happens to those who don't have stickers,' she said matter-of-factly.

'You swallow them?'

'But of course,' the Manotaur chuckled. 'I'm a ravenous man-eating Manotaur. It's in my nature.'

'But I don't want to be eaten!'

'Should've thought about that before you turned down the sticker. Come on, in you get then.'

'Wait!' I cried. 'You can't eat me!'

'Oh really? Why's that?'

'Because…er…because…' I searched frantically for an answer, and suddenly recalled the last piece of advice the strange chicken man had shouted at me from the crouton. 'Because I'm a chicken!'

The Manotaur very slowly looked me up and down. 'No you're not.'

'I am too.'

'You look nothing like a chicken. They've got feathers round the front, and a zipper at the back.'

'Mine fell off.'

The Manotaur's frown deepened with suspicion. 'Where's your beak then, eh?'

'It's in the wash.'

'A likely story!' the creature scoffed. 'I put it to you that you're a boy, and further more, I mean to eat you.'

'Aha!' I cried, pointing a victorious finger. 'If I'm a boy, then you can't eat me because you're a *man*-eater, see? So there!'

The Manotaur's massive jaw stammered open and shut. 'Blast!' she cursed. 'Another potential victim let off on a technicality.'

She produced a soggy book of stickers, tore one off which stated: 'I *wasn't* eaten alive by a ravenous man-eating Manotaur' and stuck it to my forehead.

'Be sure to stop by again in about ten years,' she hollered, as I beat a hasty retreat. 'We'll do lunch!'

8

Plight Of The Mushroom Men

Although I may have narrowly avoided being eaten by a Manotaur (and had the sticker to prove it), everything else in the swamp had had a go. By the time I'd dragged myself to the edge, I was covered from head to foot in insect bites and soaked to the skin.

Sniffling and sneezing, I trudged onwards until my path was once again blocked; this time by a massive ceramic barrier, hundreds of feet high and many miles wide.

This next soup came in its own protective dish (with the foul stench of oxtail reeking away on its doorstep, who could blame it?).

It was too tall to climb, and too wide to go around.

Fortunately I discovered a doorbell in the side, under a large sign that read: *'Ring here for service.'*

I gave it a push and waited, shivering away.

Eventually, a stuffy voice responded through the intercom: 'Soup's off! You'll have to try elsewhere.'

'I don't feel so good,' I coughed.

'Of course you don't,' the voice said stiffly. 'That's pure oxtail you've come through. You're probably carrying all manner of diseases.'

'It's just a bit of a cold,' I sniffled.

'Oh really? What colour's your tongue?'

I poked it out and had a look. 'Purple.'

'How about your lips? Any swelling?'

I glanced downwards, and noticed my bottom lip jutting out like a diving board. 'A little.'

'And your kneecaps?' insisted the voice. 'How do your kneecaps feel?'

I bent over, and gave them a gentle squeeze. 'Sore.'

'Yes, I'm not surprised. They'll be flying off in a minute, I expect. Oh well. Once your kneecaps explode, there really is very little anyone can do for you. Good day!'

'Can't you do something *before* they explode?'

'No, no, absolutely out of the question. My hands are tied on this one, I'm afraid.' The voice paused a moment in thoughtful contemplation, and then added: 'Unless…'

'Unless *what?*' I cried. 'Tell me!'

'No, it's too much to ask. Too much responsibility for one so young...'

'Just tell me what you want me to do.'

'Very well.' The person at the other end of
the intercom cleared his throat. 'You must wear
the chicken outfit.'

'Excuse me?'

'No time to argue, I'm sending one down.'

The intercom fell silent, and a large barrel
was lowered on a rope, with a small chicken
suit contained inside.

'Well?' urged the voice. 'Try it on.'

I lifted the ragged feathery costume, and
gave it a critical look. 'How will this help me
get better?'

'No time to explain. Your kneecaps could
go at any moment. Quick, hop in and try it
on.'

Spurred on by the voice, I climbed into the
barrel, scrambled out of my oxtail-soiled cloth-
ing, and slipped into the chicken outfit. It was a
snug fit, though I felt none the better for wearing it. The musty smell of feathers set me off
sneezing again.

The barrel jerked upwards, and after a few
short moments I found myself stood on top of

the soup dish, being greeted by a strange grey-skinned man with mushrooms sprouting out of his face.

'I am Doctor Funnelcap, saviour of the Mushroom Men,' he stated grandly. 'And I must say you cut a rather dashing figure in that suit.'

'I don't feel very dashing,' I grumbled.

'Nonsense, you're an angel in the guise of poultry,' the doctor grinned. 'Now, let's get you down into that soup before you catch your death of knees.'

I was led down a series of rope ladders and bridges towards the creamy white soup-pool that lay at the dishes bottom. The soup itself was deserted; the shy inhabitants watched me from the windows of large mushroom dwellings, whispering in excited voices as I passed.

'Praise be! Another chicken!'

'We're saved!'

'It's a miracle!'

I lowered myself into the warm, refreshing soup and began to paddle up and down as best as the chicken suit would allow. It was tough going at first, but I soon got the hang of it.

'That's it, lad. Swim,' the doctor encouraged. 'Swim as if your life depends upon it. Oh, and here.' He tossed me an empty thermos flask. 'Fill it up, and drink as much as you like. You are, after all, the key ingredient.'

'Eh?'

'Never mind, never mind.'

Smiling a little too widely, the doctor left me swimming in the soup.

It was good stuff! The more I drank, the better I felt. Within seconds, my kneecaps stopped throbbing, my nose stopped streaming; even the insect bites lost their sting.

Gradually the soup around me filled with mushroom men, who leapt in from diving boards attached to the fronts of their houses.

Soon the soup heaved with activity. Everywhere I looked there were lumpy-headed people splashing around, bathing, surfing and having a good time. Those sombre grey faces I'd observed watching from the windows earlier had been banished forever, replaced by expressions of joy and mirth.

I too joined in the revelry, launching myself off diving boards, tumbling down slides, slicing through the waters on soup skis (to the casual observer I must have looked a most peculiar sight, skimming through the soup in a chicken outfit).

Rather than tiring me out, all this activity made me feel stronger and healthier than ever before. I was certainly strong enough to resume my quest. I hauled myself out onto a wooden platform, and looked around for the exit.

Instantly the mushroom men stopped swimming, and let out exasperated cries.

'The chicken has forsaken us!' they wailed.

'We're doomed! *Doomed!*'

The doctor hurried down a rope ladder, and rushed to my side.

'Feeling better?'

'Much, thanks. Though I probably best be heading off.'

'Why leave?' the doctor said, chuckling nervously. 'This is paradise. I challenge you to find a more wondrous soup.'

'I'm not looking for soup, I'm looking for my Grandpa's teeth.'

'Well perhaps they're here someplace?' enthused the doctor.

'I don't think so. Thanks all the same.'

'Don't go!' the doctor pleaded. 'We need you. Things haven't been the same since our last chicken ran off. After all, what use is chicken and mushroom soup without a chicken to provide flavour?'

'But I'm not a real chicken.'

'Ah, but the soup doesn't know that,' said Doctor Funnelcap slyly. 'Soup's *thick*. And rather tasty, too.' He unfastened the cap on his thermos, scooped it through the soup, and took a long swig. 'Drink enough of this wonderful stuff and you'll never get ill, you'll never grow old, and you'll never die. Think about it…it's a grand opportunity, lad. With disease-ridden oxtail soup to one side, and the cold arctic wastes of gazpacho to the other, we're never short of sickly customers willing to pay ridiculous prices for our miracle cure. All we need do to provide it is laze around in a pool all day, having a fabulous time. Doesn't that sound terrific?'

'If it's so great,' I said, narrowing my eyes in suspicion, 'why don't *you* put on the chicken outfit?'

A sharp collective intake of breath went up from the mushroom bathers.

'Blasphemy!' they hissed. 'Blasphemy!'

'And have a mushroom dressed as chicken?' the doctor roared. 'It would be a crime against nature! The very idea…'

He placed a firm hand on my shoulder, bony fingers digging in sharply through the feathers. 'No, you must stay here with us, forever and ever and ever!'

9

Gazpacho Chills

I left as soon as darkness fell.
Although an eternal life of laziness sounded tempting at first, the prospect of spending it dressed in a chicken suit did not.

Once the soup was deserted I slipped from the pool and crept through the shadows, stealthily making my way up rope ladders and bridges, past lifeguard towers containing ever-watchful mushroom men.

Finally I reached the safety of the dishes rim.

A chill breeze drifted across from the vast gazpacho wasteland that lay beyond, rippling my costume's feathers and sending a shiver down my spine.

Spotting a large empty barrel dangling over the edge, I climbed inside and lowered myself down.

The soup below was like one massive red ice-rink, glistening in the moonlight. Penguins skated across its surface, weaving in and out of one another, gliding along with grace and ease.

I skidded awkwardly along behind them, sometimes on my feet, mostly on my face.

With a disapproving chitter, the penguins left me sliding alone in the darkness, having clearly decided that although I was dressed as a bird, I was not one of them.

Fierce arctic winds howled around me. Icicles formed on the end of my beak, but still I pressed on; one lone chicken against a harsh and hostile wilderness.

Whenever the cold got too much, I uncapped my thermos and took a long swig. Hot soup coursed through my body, banishing the chills and giving me the burst of strength I needed.

I caught sight of a campfire flickering away in the distance, and clambered up the icy rocks towards it.

As I approached, I could hear voices arguing in the darkness.

'Whose bright idea was it to take the celery soup channel?'

'I didn't hear no one complainin' at the time,' retorted a second voice. '"A mosht magnifishent short cut", you shaid.'

'It seems less magnificent now the ship's stuck in celery,' snapped the first voice, 'and we're marooned here, suckin' soup popsicles in the dark.'

'Well how wash I shupposhed ter know the shoup wash condenshed?' grumbled the second voice. 'That shtuff'sh thicker than treacle! It'll take nothin' short of a monshoon ter shift it.'

'Never mind, eh, Captain?' chimed a third voice. 'Have another lolly.'

'I don't want a lolly!' snapped the Captain. 'I wantsh me teesh back!'

The Captain leant forwards into the flickering light of the campfire, and gurned moodily at his crewmates. Even without his shining white

teeth I'd recognise that ugly bearded face any-
where. It was none other than the insidious
Captain Crabcakes and his motley band of
pirates.

Well, we were on dry land now, and the
soup was far too solid for him to push me into. I
decided to step forward and give the Captain a
piece of my mind.

'Now look here,' I began. Before I could
finish, someone cried: 'Bless my scabs, a giant
chicken!' and I was seized by rough hands and
wrestled to the ground.

'Exshellent work, ladsh,' hollered the
Captain. 'We'll dine heartily tonight.'

'Hold yer seahorses, Cap'ain,' said one of
the pirates, as he tugged the headpiece off my
chicken outfit. 'That's no chicken. It's that
Gribble Grobble hunter we met earlier.'

The Captain yanked me to my feet, and leant in close to my face. 'Where were you in my hour of need, eh?'

'Drowning in pea soup, thanks to you,' I countered. 'What happened to your teeth?'

'What do yer think happened?' the Captain said bitterly. 'Gribble Grobblesh got 'em.'

'But you sail in soup, and they hunt in custard.'

The Captain stifled a cough, and scratched the back of his lice-infested locks. 'Ar, it'sh me own darned fault fer holdin' a cushtard pie fight.'

My eyebrows raced each other to the top of my head. 'A what?'

'It'sh an ancient nautical tradition. Y'shee, from time to time we get together with all the other piratesh who shail the Sheven Shoups, arm up our cannonsh and fire cushtard piesh at one another. There'sh a lot of shkill involved, and it'sh devilish good fun ter boot!'

'Arrr!' murmured the pirate crew, scraping frozen teardrops from their eyes. 'You should see that custard fly...'

'Anyway, it wash all going well, and we were rackin' up quite a shcore, when shuddenly, from out of nowhere, I wash shmacked full in the face by the biggesht cushtard pie you ever did shee. Before I knew what wash happening, a Gribble Grobble'sh tentacle whipped out and had it away with me teesh. We've been purshuin' the curshed beasht ever shince.'

I squinted at the Captain's dribble-encrusted face. 'But your teeth are real, aren't they?'

The Captain accepted a soup-lolly from one of his crew and wrapped his gummy lips around it. 'Doeshn't shtop a Gribble Grobble. If they takesh a fanshy to yer choppersh, they're comin' out, real or not!'

I clamped both feathery hands over my mouth in horror. Although I'd been trying to lose my teeth for years so I could be just like my dear Grandpa, I certainly didn't want a Gribble Grobble grabbing them.

'Oh, don't worry, I should think you'll be perfectly shafe. You've got more holesh than teesh anyway, an' them Gribble Grobblesh have got their shtandardsh, after all.'

I lowered my hands and breathed a sigh of relief.

The Captain sucked casually at his lolly. 'No, they'll probably jusht eat you an' be done with it.'

'T-t-they eat people?' I stammered.

'Whaddayer think they need all thoshe teesh for, eh?' The Captain gnashed his wet gums emphatically together. 'Chompin' and chewin' through all that ghashtly grishtle!'

The thought of Grandpa's glorious gnashers being put to such misuse filled me with cold dread. His false teeth could bite through any-thing! No creature was safe, as long as the Gribble Grobble had them in its possession.

'Here, you'll be needing thish.' The Captain tossed me a harpoon gun with a plunger on the end, fixed to a length of rope. 'Fire it at the creaturesh gob, and yank those choppersh free. Besht get them before they get you, eh?'

I shouldered the weapon, and glanced from pirate to pirate. 'Aren't you coming with me?'

They stared at their feet, and sucked intently at their lollies.

'No shense in us all gettin' et,' reasoned the Captain. 'Eshpecially when we've got you to do all the dirty work.'

Typical! Without the reassuring feel of a firm ship beneath their feet, these pirates were bigger cowards than Gribble Grobbles.

'Looks like I'm not the only chicken around here,' I grumbled, as I set off once more into the arctic wilderness.

10

The Dreaded Minestrone

Cold, alone, and armed only with a plunger, I trudged towards my fate.

The last trickle of chicken and mushroom soup dripped between my parched, frozen lips, and I cast the empty thermos aside.

I was out of soup, and my courage was fading fast, when a faint voice called to me on the wind.

'Keep going, lad. You're almost there!'

It was my Grandpa's voice. He needed me. Bracing myself against the raging blizzard, I forced my feet onwards, leaving three-toed chicken prints fading behind me in the snow.

Finally, the snowstorm broke, and I stepped out onto an icy precipice. Below lay an enormous black lagoon of minestrone. The first rays of a new day attempted to radiate grandly off its surface, but were instead sucked into its gloopy depths.

There was something about this soup that made me feel uneasy. Strange ripples formed on its surface, and large frothy air bubbles floated to the top, like something deep down was breathing.

Every instinct urged me to turn back…Run away now, before it was too late.

'Well?' said a voice. 'What are you waiting for?'

I cupped both wings to my lips and cried: 'Grandpa? Is that you?'

'Of course it's me,' replied the distant voice. 'Why wouldn't it be me, eh?'

'What are you doing in soup?' I asked.

The voice fell silent a moment, and then answered: 'Well, obviously it's not *all* of me in here. Just me teeth…Now come on in and get 'em. Be a good lad, me gobblers are gaspin'!'

Encouraged by the cheerful tone of my Grandpa's voice, I plunged into the soup. It was hideous stuff! It stung my eyes, and clung to my costume's feathers like oil to a doomed seabird. Awkwardly, I splashed onwards as the voice drew me further and further away from shore.

'That's it, keep going. Just a little further now.'

I glanced back over my shoulder. The icy realm of gazpacho was little more than a pale speck on the horizon. Dark storm clouds gathered above. A distant peal of thunder rumbled out a warning.

'Hold on a minute,' I said, as a sudden thought occurred to me. 'If it's just your teeth down there, how are they talking?'

A thoughtful silence descended, into which the smug voice replied: 'Ventriloquism! I was a master in my youth. Did I forget to mention that?'

'Yes,' I said, growing suspicious, 'you did.'

'Well I'm mentioning it now. Look, there isn't much time – the Gribble Grobble's sleeping. Now's your chance to pull my chompers free. Dive, lad. Dive!'

Against my better judgement, I took a deep breath and dived.

'Getting warmer...' the voice encouraged, as I sunk deeper and deeper into the foul waters. 'Warmer...Oooh, you're practically on fire.'

My feet touched down on the murky soup bed, and I squinted through the gloom.

Up ahead lay a massive cave, where the Gribble Grobble no doubt lay sleeping. Around it, hundreds of pairs of false teeth of all shapes and sizes were scattered like rocks.

Cautiously I picked my way through the gigantic dental graveyard, searching for my Grandpa's most prized possession.

As I stepped over a pair of dentures I noticed it twitch ever so slightly.

For a moment I thought my eyes were playing tricks, but then as my foot came close, another pair of false teeth slithered out of my path.

Something strange was going on here.

Heart racing, fear welling up inside, I carefully traced the faint outline of a tentacle from its tip, all the way back to the huge see-through mound it was attached to.

Suddenly the mound opened a beady eye, and then another, and another, and another and...well, after the fifty-seventh eye I lost count, but the important thing to note is they were all focused on *me*.

The Gribble Grobble wasn't sleeping after all...It was waiting for a foolish boy to stumble into its trap!

With no further need to keep up its disguise, the creature shed its camouflage. I found myself face to face with a repulsive blubbery mound of pulsating flesh, with long green tentacles sprouting on all sides. The tentacles had suckers, and inside the suckers were teeth stolen from its unfortunate victims.

In the centre of its body was the largest mouth of all; a vast, gaping chasm that could easily swallow a man or child whole. And in that mouth was the very item I'd crossed the Seven Soups and overcome countless obstacles to reclaim.

Grandpa's teeth!

'That's it, boy,' said the teeth, in a perfect imitation of my Grandpa's voice. 'This way.' The Gribble Grobble gnashed the teeth together. 'Come and give yer Grandpa's gobblers somethin' nice and crunchy to eat!'

Not only were these cunning beasts chameleons, but mimics too.

Well, this Gribble Grobble wasn't the only one with a trick up its sleeve. Shaking off the terror that had momentarily frozen me to the spot, I lifted my harpoon gun, took careful aim, and fired.

TWANG!

The plunger drifted lazily through the thick soup. By the time it reached the creature's mouth, it had almost slowed to a standstill. The Gribble Grobble yawned theatrically, closed its teeth around the plunger, and crunched it into tiny pieces.

Then it began to suck in the rope attached to the plunger, like it was a long strand of spaghetti. As I was slowly dragged towards it, I realised grimly that I was the unfortunate meat-ball attached to the other end.

For a moment I considered letting go of the harpoon gun, but this was the only chance I had.

At the very last second I pulled sharply backwards, planted my feet against the warty area beneath its lower lip, and tugged the rope as hard as I could.

The false teeth gave a wobble.

The Gribble Grobble sucked with added gusto, drawing in great greedy mouthfuls of minestrone. There was no doubt in my mind that this beast would gladly drain the whole lagoon to get to me.

I teetered perilously on the edge of its massive mouth, sucked one way, pulling another, locked in one almighty game of tug of war. If I won, I'd have my Grandpa's teeth. If I lost, the Gribble Grobble would have its meal.

Well, I wasn't about to let that happen. If I got et by Grandpa's teeth he'd never forgive himself!

Slowly, inch-by-inch, I worked those choppers free.

The creature lashed out with its tentacles, snapping away with its teeth, but it was too late.

I gave one last desperate tug and **POP!** The false teeth shot from its mouth like a cork from a bottle, straight into my waiting hands.

I paddled frantically to the surface, and broke the crest of the soup, gasping for air.

Rain lashed down from billowing clouds above. Wind tossed me from side to side. The shore was a tiny speck on the horizon. I thrashed away with my feet, Grandpa's teeth held out before me like a giant toothy float.

With a huge ear-splitting roar the Gribble Grobble surfaced behind me, and gave chase.

That massive mouth, which had previously held my Grandpa's teeth, gaped wide open, swallowing everything in its path.

I kicked harder and faster, but the beast was gaining. Soon the false teeth would be back in its mouth, and I'd be trapped behind them in that ghastly cavernous maw!

A tentacle curled around my foot and hauled me from the water, when suddenly —

SH-LUUKK!

A plunger raced down, and plucked a shining white pair of teeth from the tentacle's suckers.

The Gribble Grobble dropped me and let out a frenzied howl, which was immediately silenced by a rain of plungers.

SH-LUUCK! SH-LUUCK! SH-LUUCK! SH-LUUCK! SH-LUUUCK!

Every one of them hit their mark, ripping dentures from the beast's writhing limbs.

I looked up through the churning waters, and saw a pirate ship cresting the waves. Captain Crabcakes stood upon the bow, giving me a pearly white grin. 'Avast, ye lubber!' he bellowed. 'We'll show you who's chicken!'

Cannons fired. Plungers soared through the air. The Gribble Grobble wailed as every last one of its precious dentures were mercilessly tugged free.

Deprived of its lunch and the means with which to eat it, the beast let out one last lisping, salivary roar, and sunk into the ocean.

Whooping and cheering, the pirate crew brought their ship around, and helped me aboard.

'Ahoy there, matey!' cried Captain Crabcakes, beaming away as he stood atop a massive pile of plundered teeth. 'Thanks fer actin' as bait whilst we prised our ship free.'

'Don't mention it,' I grumbled. It wasn't much fun being bait, especially when there were pirates ready to step in at the last moment and hog all the glory.

'Well, I must say this is a fine toothy booty we've landed ourselves here, lads,' Captain Crabcakes enthused. 'We'll be the envy of all who sail upon the Seven Soups.'

Some of the gummier crew members had already started rummaging in the pile, trying out teeth for size.

'Ugh! This one tastes like fish paste!' said one pirate, spitting a yellow pair clear across the deck.

I stumbled after them, and prodded them gingerly with a toe. 'I think these belong to a troll I met. I'm sure he'd be grateful for their return.'

'How grateful?' asked Captain Crabcakes, stroking his maggot-dappled beard thoughtfully.

'He'd pay you in clams,' I said. 'Perhaps as many as twelve, if you haggle.'

'Arrr, been years since I've had a nice clam chowder. Where's this rascal live?'

'Tomato soup. And whilst you're heading that way,' I added, 'any chance you could drop me off in custard?'

'I can do better than that, lad.' The Captain delved into the pocket of his waistcoat, and produced a packet of instant custard. 'Had some left over from our ill-fated sea battle. Won't be needin' this again.' He tore it open, and tipped it over the side.

One of the pirates took up an oar, and stirred the custard round and round.

'That's it, lad. Give it a good stir!' encouraged the Captain. 'Don't let that minestrone get the upper hand.'

I approached the edge of the ship, and prepared to step into the custard whirlpool. 'Well, I
guess I'll be off then.'

Captain Crabcakes placed a restraining hand
on my shoulder. 'I'll do the honours, if yer
don't mind.'

Before I could protest, he planted a boot on
my rump, and kicked me into the ocean.

'Don't forget to tell all yer friends Captain
Crabcakes is a right old stinker!' cackled the
dastardly pirate, as I was sucked under into the
custard.

11

Grandpa Gets His Gnashers Back

'Argh! A custard-drizzled Chicken Man!' cried the Major, as I resurfaced in the barrel. 'Quick, fetch my musket.'

A wrinkled hand reached down, and hauled me out. 'Thatsh no chicken,' lisped Grandpa. 'Thatsh my grandshon.'

'And these, I believe, are your teeth,' I said, kneeling down in a pool of custard to present him with his most magnificent gnashers.

'Blesh you, my dear boy. Blesh you!' With trembling fingers, Grandpa forced his teeth between gummy lips. His wrinkled face smoothed out to make way for a grin of gargantuan proportions. 'Just think m'boy, one day all this will be yours.'

'I'll probably just start brushing my teeth actually, Grandpa,' I said, giving him a sheepish smile. After all, it seemed to me that false teeth required a lot of effort and could get a fellow into rather deep custard if he wasn't careful.

Miss Skillet bustled into the dining room and propped the door back. 'Ah, you found them then? Jolly good. Just in time for breakfast.' She placed an extra large glass of water down at Grandpa's side. 'Pop those hideous things out into the glass, and I'll bring soup.'

'But I've only just popped them in,' Grandpa grumbled.

Oblivious to his cries of protest, she stalked off towards the food preparation room.

'All's well that ends well,' said Dad.

'Let's get you into a nice hot bath,' said Mum, giving my soggy custard and soup stained chicken costume a disapproving look.

Suddenly there came a most horrendous crash that shook the building to its very foundations. We rushed into the food preparation area, and discovered the Gnashomatic 4500 lay in smoking ruins. Gears and pistons squealed uselessly away, with nothing left to power.

Its metal teeth had vanished.

'My machine!' Miss Skillet sobbed. 'My precious machine!'

Out of the corner of my eye I caught sight of a long green tentacle slithering away into a vat of custard, with something large and metallic glinting in its grasp.

The Gribble Grobble had returned for second helpings.

'Don't worry, my darlings,' cried Miss Skillet. 'I'll save you!'

She leapt headfirst into the vat of custard, never to be seen again.

'Looks like soup's off the menu,' said Grandpa, gnashing his teeth merrily.

A cheer rippled through the pensioners' ranks, and false teeth were hurriedly slipped back into gummy mouths. Moments later, the dining room was flooded with the most incredible amount of crunching, gnashing, chewing, grinding, chomping and biting, as one by one the ravenous pensioners worked their way through every item the Gnashomatic's mighty choppers had missed.

Grandpa sat before them at the head of the table with a towering mound of mussels, oyster shells, ostrich eggs, coconuts, celery sticks, lobsters, and various other crunchable foodstuffs piled to the ceiling on his plate.

'Show us yer teeth! Show us yer teeth! Show us yer teeth!' chanted the urchins from outside, their grubby faces pressed up against the window.

And no one in the world, not even the most powerful of psychics could possibly have predicted what Grandpa Grynbad was going to gobble next.

About The Author

David Hailwood used to write whilst hanging upside-down by his legs, from a tree. Now he's an adult he's apparently not allowed to do that sort of thing any more, so instead he sits at home in his office, cackling manically at his computer (occasionally he remembers to switch it on).

With over twenty years experience working in the UK comics market, his brain matter has leaked onto the pages of numerous comic anthologies, including Egmont's best selling children's comic 'Toxic'.

He has written comedy material for the BBC, ITV and E4, and once starred in a short comedy horror film titled 'Attack Of The Mutant Sock Freaks', in which a bunch of deranged killer mutant socks attempt to destroy Bognor Regis.

If you've enjoyed reading this book, please take a moment to leave a review on Amazon; even if it's just a few short lines it can go a long way towards encouraging the author to write more mad stuff, and helps other readers to discover the book.

Visit the author's website at the cunningly titled **www.davidhailwood.com** and register for a newsletter to get freebies, special offers and to be kept up-to-date with new releases.

Now read on for a sneak preview of David's other thrill-packed   children's comedy fantasy: **The Last Of The Navel Navigators!**

The Last Of The
Navel Navigators

1

Deliverance

It was Erasimus T. Rigwiddle's last assignment. He was sixty years old today. Fifty-five of those years had been spent working as a courier for the Swift Wings Delivery Service, and the five years before that had been spent training to become a courier for the Swift Wings Delivery Service. As a stork, career options were extremely limited; it was either deliver babies for a living, or join the unemployment line.

So it was just as well that Erasimus loved his job. In his long, distinguished career he'd delivered babies to all five corners of planet Hotchpotch, for all manner of races. He'd delivered Sprites, Fairies, Goblins, Elves, Humans, Demi-humans, Semi-humans, Dwarves, Navigators, Orks, Sporks, Spiggots, Gollythrashers…one time he even managed to deliver a Troll. The lads back at the depot had said it couldn't be done, but by crikey he'd shown them what for!

Of course, that had been back in his younger days, before he'd become afflicted with bad hearing, a dicky heart and twenty million miles on the clock. Nowadays, even the tiny sleeping bundle secured in the delivery satchel strapped across his waist caused him to wheeze and splutter every flap of the way.

Time to retire gracefully, whilst there was still life left in this old sky-bird.

Tomorrow he would hang up his wings for good, buy a little place in the countryside and settle down with a nice lady stork. Then, if he was extremely lucky, perhaps another stork would bring them a child. A dragon, maybe. Interspecies adoption was all the rage these days – orks were adopting fairies, dwarves adopting ogres – so he didn't see why he couldn't adopt a dragon. After all, who wanted a plain old boring ordinary baby when you could have one that was multi-coloured, fire-proof and heated the house at night?

Yes, a Red Fanged Raxithorian Bird Hunting Dragon. That was the one for him! He'd have to teach it to stop hunting birds, of course. But that was all part of the joys of fatherhood. One final challenge to see him through his twilight years; was that really too much to ask?

Crrkkk! '–asimus!' a tinny voice barked in his left ear. 'This is Control! Are you reading me, over?'

'Reading you loud and clear, Control!' Erasimus piped back into his headset. 'Nothing but clear blue skies and plain sailing up ahead. Looks like I'm in for a frightfully dull end to an otherwise rip-roaring, seat of the britches, thrill packed career,' he sighed.

Crrrkt! 'Don't count your chickens whilst there's a fox on the prowl, Erasimus,' the air traffic controller crackled back. 'We have a severe weather warning! There's the mother of all storms converging on your position. And it looks like it's brought its family!'

Erasimus' eyes scanned the horizon. There was barely a cloud in the sky. 'Are you sure about that Control?'

'Absolutely certain,' the voice said sharply. 'Be advised: it's coming in fast, over.'

The light dimmed, the sky blackened and the heavens began to rumble…

'Ah, now this is more like it!' Erasimus grinned, as the rain lashed down upon him and the wind tossed him violently from side to side. 'Dashed decent of you to lay on a monsoon for me, Control. Please be sure to convey my heartiest gratitude to the Weather Wizards. They've really excelled themselves this time.'

Crrrkt! '–othing to do with the Weather Wizards, Raz. It came out of nowhere. 'Fraid I'm going to have to order you to set down immediately and return to the depot on foot.'

'What?' Erasimus shrieked. 'Abort the mission and walk home with my bally tail feathers between my legs? Never! I'm a flyer, and proud!'

The rain was coming in thick and fast now, making Erasimus' flight goggles steam up. He could barely see the beak in front of his eyes, let alone the ground that lay a thousand feet beneath his wings. 'Not once in my entire career have I failed to make a delivery,' he said, urging himself onwards, 'and I'm certainly not going to start now. Not on my last da –'

A fork of lightning stabbed down through the sky and struck him across the tail feathers.

The smell of cooked chicken filled the air.

His beak coughed and spluttered, his wings seized up.

Suddenly he was falling.

'Mayday! Mayday!' Erasimus cried. 'I'm going down!' A thick plume of smoke trailed out behind him. 'Cargo has been lost! Repeat, cargo has been lost!'

Below him, the delivery satchel tumbled end over end, its singed and tattered strap flailing helplessly in the wind. From inside there came a noise, growing louder and louder and louder.

It was the sound of a baby crying.

'I'm coming, lad!' Erasimus hollered. He pointed his beak downwards, and launched into a dive. 'Just you stay put now.'

His only hope was to reach the satchel before it hit the ground. Then perhaps at the moment before impact he could cushion it with his own frail body.

'By Jove, what a dashingly heroic way to punch one's ticket,' Erasimus enthused. 'The gods must be smiling on me today!'

G-force rippled his feathers. His scarf whipped around like a crazed King Cobra.

Just when he was so close he could almost touch the satchel with the tip of his wing, something wholly unexpected happened.

The satchel began to glow bright blue.

'Oh!' Erasimus said, barely able to keep the sense of wonder out of his voice. 'You're one of those sort of babies are you?'

With a brilliant explosion of light and a deafening '*Whuuuuuuuuuuuuumph!*' the satchel simply winked out of existence. Where it had been mere moments before, there was nothing left but a fading trail of stars.

***

In the deep dank wilderness of Southern America's Sasquatch County, two foul-smelling dungaree-clad yahoos stood staring at a scorched delivery satchel that dangled precariously over the swamp, its strap tangled in a tree branch.

It had appeared out of thin air moments ago, and had given rise to much speculation.

'What d'you think's in it Pa?' the youngest of the two – a scraggly, buck-toothed teenager named Shawney – said, scratching his buttocks. 'Munnee?'

'Nah. Gators wouldn't be that interested in money,' the eldest – a stocky balding brute called Kleetus – responded, motioning to the beady reptilian eyes that watched patiently from under the murky waters. 'They got nuffin' to spend it on, see?'

Shawney's mouth split into a grin so wide that it exposed all seven of his yellowed teeth.

'They could use it to buy shoes, Pa!' he yelled. 'Gator shoes. To replace the ones them poachers keep stealin'.'

Kleetus rolled his eyes at the heavens. 'Shawney,' he growled, 'don't make me fetch yer Ma now, y'hear?'

Shawney glanced warily at the hefty stick leant up against a tree next to Kleetus. It was seven feet long, thick as a tree trunk and had the word 'Ma' etched lovingly into its side. 'I'll be quiet, Pa,' he whispered.

'Atta boy, Shawney.'

As something began to move around inside, the satchel started to bob up and down on the branch. Kleetus and Shawney watched with renewed interest.

The branch creaked ominously.

'It's gonna fall, Pa,' Shawney said.

'Yup.'

'We prob'ly oughta do somethin'.'

'Yup.'

'We could always throw rocks at it,' Shawney suggested.

'Nope.' Kleetus picked up his stick and strode towards the edge of the bank. 'Got me a better idea.' He leant out as far as he could, stretched out an arm and hooked the strap with the end of the stick. Carefully he drew the satchel back across the water. The gators snapped at it as it passed by overhead, as if to say 'oi!' and 'that's my lunch!'

When it was safely within Kleetus' grasp he placed the satchel down on the ground, plunged in his thick, hairy arms and rummaged around inside. His fingers closed around something warm and soft.

'What is it, Pa?' Shawney asked, attempting to catch a glimpse over his father's broad shoulders. 'Food? Riches?'

'No Shawney, it's a…it's a…' Kleetus slowly drew his hands out of the satchel. Cradled within them was a newborn baby boy. He had been wrapped in a bright yellow blanket that had 'express delivery' stamped upon it in red. 'It's a buh…a buh…a buh –' Kleetus stammered, as the baby stared up at him through big, curious eyes.

'A big pink jellybean!' Shawney cried.

'Not quite, son,' Kleetus said, regaining his composure. 'What we have here is a real live genuine baby.'

Shawney leant in closer and inspected the child. He let out a guffaw. 'No wonder his parents didn't want him,' he snorted. 'He's only got ten fingers, and none of his toes are webbed!'

'Poor little tyke,' Kleetus said, as the baby attempted to suck at Shawney's eleventh finger, and spat it back out, realising something wasn't right. 'Looks hungry.'

'We got some cheeseburgers back at the ranch,' Shawney said.

Kleetus' eyes widened as the alarm bells of unexpected fatherhood sounded in his mind. 'Now hold on there, Shawney!' he said sternly. 'We can't possibly keep 'im. Bringin' up a child takes a lot of responsibility. He's not like them chickens I brought yer last Christmas. Fer one thing, the chances of eggs is unlikely.'

'But no one else wants him, Pa,' Shawney whined. ''Xcept the gators, and I don't reckon they've got his best innerests at heart.'

Kleetus cast his eyes around the swamp. There was no one else around for miles; Ma's reputation had made sure of that. 'You got a point there, son,' Kleetus said, eyeing the child thoughtfully. It gurgled at him, and blew a snot bubble. For Kleetus that was the deal clincher. 'I guess it would be useful to have a spare pair o' hands around the house, fer doin' chores and the like.'

'Them dishes still need doing, Pa,' Shawney said brightly.

'I don't think he's quite ready fer the dishes yet, Shawney,' Kleetus said, gently placing the baby back in the satchel and fastening it up. 'We'll start him on the smaller jobs first. Gator wrestlin' and that.' He grabbed the satchel by the strap and hoisted it over his shoulder.

'What we gonna call him, Pa?' Shawney asked, as they stomped their way through the undergrowth, heading back towards their weather-beaten shack.

'Don't rush me, Shawney,' Kleetus said. 'I only just got round ta namin' you.'

Prepare yourself for the ultimate hillbilly bellybutton odyssey!

Discovered in a swamp and raised by hillbillies, Jellybean 'Gator Bait' Skratcher leads a sheltered life, until he accidentally tears a hole in the fabric of the universe, whilst attempting to remove fluff from his bellybutton.

He sets off on an epic adventure across hostile worlds teeming with ravenous demons and mischievous beard pixies, all the while led by a scatterbrained stork who's made it his mission in life to deliver Jellybean to the right parents, or die trying.

But when your best friend's a goat, and your greatest hope for survival relies solely upon a talentless magician who can't even do proper card tricks, *nothing* is likely to go as planned!

Check it out on Amazon now.

Printed in Great Britain
by Amazon

32842039R00061